Eerie Encounters

Written by Judy Waite
Illustrated by Danny Flynn,
David Kearney and Mark Oldroyd

Contents

Creepy Kane 3

Knight of the Road 24

Crash Landing 46

Creepy Kane

It was the first day of Gemma's holiday.
Well, it was supposed to be a holiday.
She'd come to stay with Auntie Chris
and her cousin, Kane. Mum had gone
to look after Gran because she'd had
an operation.

Auntie Chris had this big idea that
Kane and Gemma would get on well
together. But as she got out of the taxi
and walked towards the dark, creepy-
looking house, Gemma wasn't so sure.

She had only ever met Auntie Chris and Kane once, years and years ago at a wedding. She couldn't remember much about them. But they must be a bit weird if they were happy to live in a creepy house like this.

Gemma took a deep breath and lifted her hand to knock on the door. It swung open suddenly, and she found herself staring at a tall, thin-faced boy.

"I suppose you're Gemma. I'm Kane," he said in a strange, whispery voice. "Mum said I had to let you in."

"It's nice to meet you." Gemma gave Kane a friendly smile, but he just stared at her. He didn't even offer to take her bag.

"You have to go upstairs," he said. "Mum's out at the moment. I have to show you your room."

Kane walked away towards the
staircase. Gemma followed him. The
stairs were rickety and old. Gemma
struggled up with her bag, gripping the
handrail. It felt odd – sort of cold and
dry. Then she felt something move
beneath her fingers. Gemma screamed,
and her bag crashed to the floor. For
there, wound round the handrail, was
a snake!

"Get it away!" she screamed.
"Get it away!"

But Kane just gave her a small, sly smile. "Are you scared?" he asked.

Gemma's hands were shaking, but she didn't want Kane to know how terrified she was. She had a horrible feeling that he was enjoying this.

"Of course not," she muttered. "It's not what I expected to see, that's all."

"Her name's Zora." Kane gave a slow, hissing laugh. "She's my best friend."

"Will she bite?"

Kane gave Gemma another sly smile. "Only if you frighten her. Only if you scream again." He carefully unwound Zora from the handrail and held her out towards Gemma. "Here – do you want to hold her?"

"Er, no thanks," said Gemma, trying to stop her voice from trembling.

Kane let Zora wind herself around his thin, white arm. "Mum thinks I've got a problem because I never have any friends round from school, but she's wrong." He watched Gemma carefully. "I'd just rather be with Zora than anyone else."

Gemma stared at Zora. Zora stared back. She was swaying slightly. Her forked, red tongue darted out from between her jaws, as if she was tasting the air. Flick. Flick. Flick.

Gemma tried hard to think of something to say. "She's an interesting colour, but her eyes are strange. They're sort of fuzzy and pale. Is she blind?"

"She's been shedding her skin," said Kane. "All snakes do it. Their eyes go milky-white, and the dead skin peels off from the head. It turns inside out until all of the skin is completely separate from the snake." As he spoke, Kane bent down to pick something up. It was thin and papery. He held it out to Gemma.

"Um – it's very interesting. It looks a bit like dried glue."

Gemma backed away down the stairs and picked up her bag. The thought of touching peeled snakeskin was almost as bad as touching the snake itself.

At that moment, the front door burst open. "Kane! What are you doing, bringing that snake downstairs? That's no welcome for poor Gemma, is it?"

Gemma turned to where Auntie Chris was staggering in through the door with bags of shopping. Gemma was relieved to see that she didn't look creepy at all. She wasn't like Kane.

Auntie Chris smiled at Gemma. "I'm sorry I wasn't here to greet you. I had to nip out and get some food for our supper." She put her shopping down on the floor and gave Gemma a quick hug. Then she turned back to Kane. "Now take Gemma up to her room, and put that snake away. You won't need it this week. You've got Gemma for company now. I'll go and get the supper started."

Kane didn't answer, but Gemma couldn't miss the angry look on his face before he turned to lead her upstairs.

Later that evening, after pizza and chips, and a game of Snakes and Ladders that Kane insisted they played, Gemma went to bed. She hated the room. It was full of junk. There were boxes and bags stacked everywhere. There wasn't any carpet on the floor. Gemma wished she was back home in her warm, friendly room with the pretty curtains, and all her soft toys and books.

She stared up at the ceiling, watching a long, thin cobweb sway from the dusty lampshade. The night seemed to stretch on, and on, and on. Suddenly, Gemma heard a sound. It was coming from outside her room. She stiffened. The sound came nearer and nearer, low and slithering. There was only one thing it could be – Zora!

Gemma looked towards the door. There was a gap underneath. The snake could easily slither through it. Then Gemma would be alone in the room with her. Trapped.

The shuffling sound stopped. The silence was worse. Maybe Zora was already in the room. Maybe now, from somewhere in the shadows, she was watching Gemma. Swaying slightly. Tasting the air with her tongue. Flick. Flick. Flick.

Gemma couldn't stand it any longer. She had to get away from there. She got out of bed, slowly. Keeping her back pressed against the wall, she edged her way to the door. Her feet were cold on the bare floorboards. Then, her toes touched something long and thin – Zora!

Gemma tried hard not to scream. She stumbled forward, trying to get away. She reached for the light switch and flicked it on, her eyes still locked onto the place where she had trodden on Zora. And then, as the light filled the room, she almost laughed. It wasn't Zora at all. It was just a bit of rope spilling out from one of the boxes.

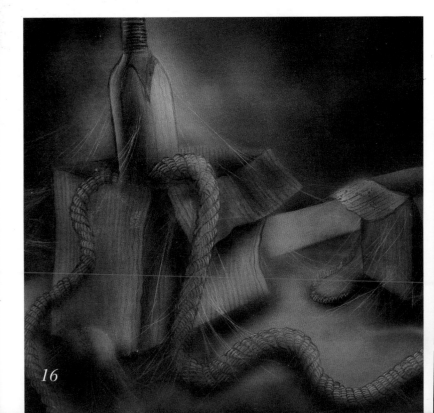

Gemma sighed and shook her head. She was so jumpy. She was getting into a state about nothing. The only good thing was that she hadn't screamed. At least she hadn't woken anybody up.

She decided to get a drink of water. Then, five minutes later, she was back in bed. This time, she kept the light on. She didn't want to lie in the dark anymore.

Gemma reached down to pull the bedclothes up tighter – and it was then that she saw it. There, lying on top of the bed, was something so frightening, so terrible, that her blood ran cold in her veins.

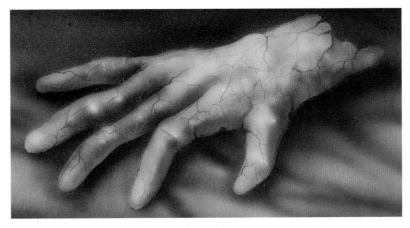

It was skin. Gemma recognised it. It was thin and papery – just like the snakeskin Kane had picked up earlier. But although it looked like a snakeskin, it didn't look like a snake shape. The wrinkled skin was in the shape of ... a human hand!

Then everything fell into place.
The way Kane was so crazy about Zora.
His hissing laugh. His strange, staring
eyes. This time Gemma couldn't stop
herself, she began to scream.

Auntie Chris rushed into the room,
pulling her dressing-gown around her.
"Whatever is the matter?" she asked.

"It's Kane ... he's not what you think
he is ... this skin – this hand ... "

Auntie Chris peered down at the hand, and then looked over her shoulder as Kane appeared in the doorway. "Kane? What's going on?" she asked.

Gemma looked at Kane. The skin on his hands was normal. He looked normal all over. He was even grinning a normal grin, and when he spoke, Gemma noticed the hissing sound had gone from his voice.

"It was just a joke," he said. "I got a rubber glove and covered it with glue. When it was dry, I peeled the glue off. It was just a bit of fun."

Gemma was still shaking. She turned to Auntie Chris. "Kane played a horrible trick on me, and I'm sorry, but I don't want to stay here anymore. Mum said if I really wasn't happy, I could go to Gran's house with her. I'd like to leave in the morning if you don't mind."

The next morning, Gemma was climbing into a taxi. She didn't look back at the creepy house. She wanted to forget about the whole thing. It was just as well, because if she had looked back, Gemma would have seen something she might never have been able to forget.

Kane was standing by the upstairs window. He was swaying slightly. His eyes were milky-pale and his long, red tongue was darting out from between his lips. Flick. Flick. Flick.

Knight of the Road

Dan never knew what made him borrow *Silver Knight.*

Silver Knight was a mountain bike. It belonged to his brother, Matt, and it was his pride and joy.

Matt always said *Silver Knight* was special. He said it was no ordinary bike. He rode it at seven o'clock every morning and spent twenty minutes racing along the hills and lanes. Then, when he got back, he would hose it down before getting ready for school.

Matt rode *Silver Knight* whatever the weather. He didn't care about fog, or rain, or even thunderstorms. Matt always said the bike was his best mate. He looked after *Silver Knight*, and *Silver Knight* looked after him.

But now, Matt was away on a school trip. As Dan sat, stirring his cereal slowly round the bowl, he found he was thinking about *Silver Knight* more and more.

Suddenly, Dan pushed his breakfast away and went out into the garage. He walked over to the bike. It was silver and very sporty. It had twenty-four gears and a speedo that recorded how fast you were going.

Dan ran his hands along the frame. It felt really powerful. It felt really special. It definitely didn't feel like an ordinary bike.

Suddenly, Dan grabbed the handlebars. He would take *Silver Knight* for a spin. He wouldn't go for long – just twenty minutes – the same as Matt always did. He might never get the chance to ride it again. And Matt would never know …

Silver Knight seemed to almost go off on its own. It raced along the country lanes. It skimmed through puddles and piles of wet leaves. It sped smoothly over every bounce and bump Dan could find to ride it over.

Dan zoomed past an old lady who was cycling slowly up a steep hill. He whizzed past the corner of the crossroads. With a shout of excitement, he raised the handlebars, doing a wheelie past the phone box.

Then, suddenly, he skidded, screeching
to a halt just in time. For there, just
round the corner, Dan saw the most
terrible sight he'd ever seen in his life.
A red car had crashed. It lay on its side
in the middle of the road. Just in front of
it, caught in the bumper, he could make
out the mangled handlebars of a bike.
A woman in a blue jacket was kneeling
sobbing nearby.

Dan jumped off *Silver Knight* and ran across to her. The woman was bending over someone. It looked like a boy. He had blood on his trousers, and on his jacket. Dan didn't dare to look at his face.

"Can I help?" Dan asked, quietly.

The woman didn't answer. She didn't even seem to notice he was there. Instead she just kept on sobbing.

"I'll get help. I know where there's a phone box." Dan jumped onto *Silver Knight* again, turning back the way he had come. He raced down the lane to the phone box. He ran in and dialled 999.

As Dan cycled back to the scene of the accident, a police car drove past him. A moment later, an ambulance whizzed by. At least help had arrived.

Dan sped round the corner, and then skidded to a stop again. He was almost more shocked than he had been the first time. The police car was there. The ambulance was there. But there was nothing else. There was no red car lying on its side in the middle of the road. There were no mangled handlebars caught in the bumper of the car. There was no woman sobbing over a blood-splattered boy.

Dan was stunned. His mouth hung open. He stood staring all around him.

"What's your problem, son?" asked a policeman. He looked grim-faced and angry. The ambulance was already driving away.

"I ..." Dan blinked and shook his head. "I thought there was an accident here."

The policeman snapped his notepad open. "I thought that too," he said coldly. "Who exactly did you hear it from?"

Dan suddenly realised that there was no point in telling the policeman it was him who'd phoned the police. The policeman didn't look in the mood to believe his story. He certainly wouldn't believe that there really had been an accident.

"I just heard it from some kids up the road," Dan said.

The policeman slammed his notebook shut. "If you see them again, perhaps you could tell them how much time and money they waste with these hoax calls. We could have been spending our time dealing with a real emergency, not this silly sort of prank that you youngsters find so clever."

"Yes. If I see them, I'll tell them."

Dan got back on *Silver Knight* and cycled away. But he didn't cycle fast now. He didn't spin along the country lanes. He didn't skim through the puddles. He went slowly, carefully, almost like an old lady. But although he was going slowly, his mind was racing. What had happened? Was he going mad? Was it some kind of punishment for riding *Silver Knight* when he shouldn't have?

He got back home and wheeled the bike back into the garage. He felt sick and shaky. He never wanted to ride *Silver Knight* again. And he supposed he never would. Matt was due back from the school trip that evening. He would never normally let Dan near his precious bike.

The next morning, at exactly seven o'clock, there was a shout from the garage. The kitchen door burst open, and Matt rushed in to where Dan was eating his breakfast.

"You've been using *Silver Knight*, haven't you?"

Dan went bright red. "What makes you think that?"

"It's muddy. There are splash marks on it. I would have never left it dirty like that."

"I ..." Dan tried hard to think of an excuse as to how the bike could have got into that state on its own, but he was no good at lying. "I was only trying it out."

"You shouldn't have been anywhere near it!" Matt was very angry. "You'd no right to ride it!"

"I'm sorry," Dan said helplessly.

"You will be," growled Matt. "If you've broken anything …"

"I haven't. I promise."

Matt gave him one last glare, then turned and strode back out of the house. After a moment, Dan heard the click of gears as Matt cycled off.

Dan felt miserable. He hated it when Matt was cross with him. He should have cleaned *Silver Knight* up afterwards, but he was upset and frightened about what had happened. He'd just wanted to put the bike away and not see it again.

He stirred his cereal round the bowl. He wasn't hungry anymore. Suddenly, he looked up at the clock. Half-past seven. That was odd. Matt usually only went for twenty minutes. He was late.

Five more minutes went past, and then ten. Dan's stomach began to churn. Then, everything fell into place, like a gear clicking in his head. The accident. What if it had really been some sort of warning? What if he was supposed to have stopped Matt from going?

Pushing his breakfast aside, Dan ran to the garage and grabbed his own bike. He jumped on it, puffing up the hill, past the crossroads and the phone box. As he rounded the corner, a sick feeling almost swamped him. Everything was exactly the same as before. The red car was there, lying on its side in the middle of the road. And the woman – the woman –

Dan dropped his bike onto the road and stared at her. Everything wasn't exactly the same after all. It was the same woman, but she wasn't kneeling, sobbing over a blood-splattered boy. She was walking about, thumping her fist on the bonnet of her car. Beside her stood Matt, with *Silver Knight*.

"It's these wet leaves," the woman was saying crossly. "The council should do something about them. It's lucky you were behind me, and not in front. If you'd been ahead of me, I would never have avoided you. You'd probably be lying in that gutter by now. You might even be ... "

Matt looked round as Dan moved his bike to the grass and walked over to them.

"It was lucky wasn't it?" Matt said softly. "If I hadn't stopped to have a moan at my little brother here ... " He squeezed Dan's shoulder. "I know it was a fluke," he said, "but you borrowing *Silver Knight* probably saved my life."

Dan didn't answer. Instead, he turned and looked at *Silver Knight*. He remembered Matt saying that the bike was his best mate. "I look after *Silver Knight*, and *Silver Knight* looks after me." Dan knew that somehow *Silver Knight* had wanted to make Matt late that morning. He would never be able to explain it, but saving Matt's life hadn't been a fluke at all. Matt was right. *Silver Knight* definitely wasn't an ordinary bike.

45

Crash Landing

It all started when we found the wreckage in the wood.

"Hey, look!" said Richard, running over to it. "It must be a crashed plane."

"Maybe it's from World War Two," I said, following him slowly.

"I don't think so." Richard shook his head. "I've got books about war planes, and I've never seen one that's purple and blue before. And look at those weird silver marks on the metal – they seem to be glowing. It looks like everything's still hot."

"What does that mean?" I asked, nervously.

"It means this could be a recent crash," said Richard. "It might have only just happened."

I squinted at the crumpled heap of
metal. The markings on it were
definitely strange. It wasn't just the
shimmering glow they gave off, making
them look like there was a light behind
them, it was the patterns and shapes
they were made with. They looked like
writing, but it wasn't any language I
recognised. It was like a secret code.
Still, whatever it was, I didn't like it.
It was giving me an odd feeling.

"We ought to tell someone," I said. "There might be … bodies. I'll ring the police."

I pulled Mum's mobile phone out of my pocket. She lets me borrow it sometimes. She says it's a way of checking where I am in the holidays. I tried to switch the phone on, but nothing happened.

"The battery must be flat," I said. It was strange, though. I knew Mum had only charged it up last night. I looked back at Richard. "We'd better get out of these woods. We'd better get help."

Richard shook his head. "I think we should check round," he said. "If there are people injured, we should try to find them. One of us ought to stay with them."

Richard began to search through the wreckage, pushing at it with a broken branch. After a moment, I noticed the branch was glowing. The strange light seemed to have got inside that too.

I turned away. The plane was pretty wrecked. I couldn't believe anyone had survived. And if Richard did find any bodies, I wasn't sure that I wanted to see them. And it was then that I saw it.

It was hanging on a nearby bush. I thought it was a bag at first – a black bin liner. I went nearer, wondering if it was something to do with the plane.

As I got closer, I could see that it
wasn't a bag at all. It was mushy and
slimy, like a piece of liver. Then I realised
with a sick horror that it was moving.
There was a squelching, slushing noise.
The whole thing began to split open –
and a creature slid out.

The creature was like nothing I'd ever seen before in my life. It was small – about as big as my baby sister. It was grey in colour, with a huge head and no hair. The mouth was just a slit – about two centimetres long. Its eyes were wide open, staring at me.

I started to back away. As I moved, its arm shot out as if it was trying to grab me. I was terrified, but fascinated too. It had a long, thin arm. Its hand only had four fingers. There was no thumb. I could also see that the fingers didn't have fingernails. Instead there were little sort of suction pads – a bit like those toys that you stick on the window.

Slowly, as if I was being sucked back towards it, I felt my own arm lift up and reach out towards the creature. Then I heard a scream. It was Richard.

"What on Earth is that?" he shouted, grabbing me. "Let's get out of here!"

Richard's scream seemed to wake me from a kind of trance. I turned with him, and we ran. I only looked back once. The creature was still staring at me. Its arm was still stretched out towards me.

We raced back through the woods.
We crashed through nettles and bushes,
scratching our faces and our arms. We
didn't care. We didn't even notice.

When we got to the edge of the
wood, I took the mobile out of my
pocket again. I could hardly press the
buttons, my hands were shaking so
much. But the light on the top, and the
beep, beep, beep as I pressed the
numbers, told me it was now working.

"Police! Fire! Ambulance! Anybody!"
I shouted into the mouthpiece. "There's
something in the woods. A strange blue
and purple metal thing has crashed.
There's a creature in there. It isn't an
animal. I don't know what it is ..."

After I'd finished the call, Richard and
I stood and waited. We were both
shaking. We were both crying.

It wasn't the police that came. It wasn't an ambulance, or the fire brigade, either. It was the army. A four-wheel drive jeep hurtled round the corner, then screeched to a halt beside us. Four soldiers jumped out. They didn't take any notice of us. They grabbed some equipment from the back of the jeep, and raced away into the woods.

A fifth soldier got out of the jeep. She started taking details from us.

"We thought it was a plane at first –" Richard was saying, still shaking, still crying. Suddenly, he stopped talking and buried his head in his hands. I took over from him.

"The creature was so weird. I think it was an –" Then I stopped, too. I didn't want to say it. I didn't want to tell the soldier that I thought it was an alien. I just wanted to push the whole thing out of my head.

Just then, there was crashing in the
bushes. Two of the other soldiers came
back out. They took the woman soldier
to one side. They talked together in
whispers, standing in a little huddle.

Then the female soldier came back to
us. "We've got a car coming," she said
briskly. "I'm going to take you home."

About five minutes later, a big black car turned up. The woman soldier got in the back with us, and we were driven away. Richard's mum was at work, so he came home with me.

"I'm afraid these boys have got themselves into a bit of a state," the soldier told my mum. She sounded cross, as if we were silly children who had been caught playing with matches.

"They found an – er – a crashed aeroplane, and their imaginations ran wild. I thought I'd better bring them home before they start running round telling silly stories."

The soldier gave us a long, hard look. It wasn't a kind look. It was more of a warning. It was a way of telling us not to talk about what we'd seen. And Richard, at least, seemed to go along with it.

"It was just a plane after all," said Richard later, when the soldier had gone. "I hope the pilot's all right. I expect he crawled away and was sheltering in the bushes somewhere. D'you fancy going to the park tomorrow?"

He didn't mention the alien creature. In fact, to this day, he has never mentioned any of it again. It's as if he really has managed to push it from his mind. I wish I'd been able to do that, but I haven't.

That first night I looked in the paper. I even watched the evening news on TV. There was no mention of a plane crash. And to be honest, I knew that there wouldn't be. The whole thing had been kept secret. I suppose the army thinks ordinary people shouldn't hear stories like that. I suppose they think everyone would panic if they thought there really were aliens about, crashing their spaceships in our woods. The army probably thinks it's not something ordinary people should have to worry about.

But I can't stop thinking about it.
I still see that strange grey creature,
reaching out its hand to me. I wonder
where it is now. I wonder if it's being
kept in some secret army place
somewhere. I know it sounds barmy, but
I'm almost certain that it's still alive. I'm
almost certain that it's still reaching out
to me. Every now and then, when I've
got my mum's mobile, it begins to glow.
Then, weird silver marks flash up on the
screen like a secret code. And I get the
feeling that I'm being sucked inside …